DATE DUE

AUG 1 2000

Kipper's Toybox

Requests for permission to make copies of any part of the work should be mailed to:
Permissions Department, Harcourt, Inc., 6277 Sea Harbor Drive, Orlando, Florida 32887-6777.

First published in Great Britain in 1992 by Hodder Children's Books
First hardcover U.S. edition published in 1992 by Gulliver Books/Harcourt, Inc.

First Red Wagon Books edition 2000

Red Wagon Books is a registered trademark of Harcourt, Inc.

The Library of Congress has cataloged the hardcover edition as follows:
Inkpen, Mick.
Kipper's toybox/Mick Inkpen.
p.   cm.
Summary: Kipper the dog's life changes when he discovers why there is a hole in his toybox.
[1. Dogs—Fiction.   2. Toys—Fiction.   3. Mice—Fiction.]   I. Title.
PZ7.I564Kk   1992
[E]—dc20   91-40467
ISBN 0-15-200501-3

ISBN 0-15-202427-1 pb

A C E F D B

Kipper's Toybox
Mick Inkpen

Red Wagon Books
Harcourt, Inc.
San Diego   New York   London

Someone or something had been nibbling a hole in Kipper's toybox.

"I hope my toys are safe," said Kipper. He emptied them out and counted them.

"One, two, three, four, five, six, SEVEN! That's wrong!" he said. "There should only be six!"

Kipper counted his toys again.
This time he lined them up to
make it easier.

"Big Owl one, Hippopotamus two,
Sock Thing three, Slipper four,
Rabbit five, Mr. Snake six.

"That's better!" he said.

Kipper put his toys back in the toybox. Then he counted them one more time. Just to make sure.

"One, two, three, four, five, six, seven, EIGHT noses! That's two too many noses!" said Kipper.

Kipper grabbed Big Owl and threw him out of the toybox.

"ONE!" he said crossly.

Out went Hippopotamus, "TWO!"

Out went Rabbit, "THREE!"

Out went Mr. Snake, "FOUR!"

Out went Slipper, "FIVE!"

But where was six? Where was Sock Thing?

Kipper was upset. Next to Rabbit,
Sock Thing was his favorite.
Now he was gone!

"I won't lose any more of you,"
said Kipper. He picked up the rest
of his toys and put them in his basket.
Then he climbed in and kept watch
until bedtime.

That night Kipper was awakened by a strange noise.

It was coming from the corner of the room.

Kipper turned on the light.
There, wriggling across the floor,
was Sock Thing! It must have
been Sock Thing who had been
nibbling a hole in his toybox!

Kipper was not sure what to do.
None of his toys had ever come to
life before. He jumped back in his
basket and hid behind Big Owl.

Sock Thing wriggled slowly around in
a circle and bumped into the basket.
Then he began to wriggle back the
way he had come.

He did not seem to know where
he was going. Kipper followed.

Quickly Kipper grabbed him
by the nose. Sock Thing squeaked
and wriggled harder.

Then a little tail appeared.
A little pink tail.

And a little voice said,
"Don't hurt him!"

"So it was YOU! You have been
making the hole in my toybox!"
said Kipper.

It was true. The mice had been
nibbling pieces of Kipper's toybox
to make their nest.

"You must promise not to nibble
it again," said Kipper.

"We promise," said the mice.

In return, Kipper let the mice share his basket. It was much cozier than a nest made of cardboard, and the two little mice never nibbled Kipper's toybox again....

But their babies did.
They nibbled EVERYTHING!